THE DAY OF
RODEO

BY DOROTHY AND THOMAS HOOBLER
ILLUSTRATED BY ROBERTA COLLIER-MORALES

**McGraw-Hill
School Division**

New York   Farmington

Luisa opened her eyes. A sound woke her up. Then it came again. A pebble rattled on the floor. It had come through her window.

She hopped out of bed and peeked outside. In the moonlight, she saw Juan looking up. He saw her too and put a finger to his lips. She understood. She must be quiet and not wake anyone else up.

Dressing quickly, she tiptoed down the wooden steps. Carefully, she pulled open the heavy oak front door. It was never locked. Here on the *hacienda*—the large ranch of her family, the Vallejos—there were no thieves.

Juan stood waiting. "I thought you might have changed your mind," he said.

Luisa shook her head. "No. I am ready. I want to see the rodeo on horseback."

Once a year, the *vaqueros,* or cowboys, of Mexican California rounded up the cattle. This was the time of the rodeo.

The vaqueros would need to use all their skills. They had to ride as fast as the wind. At the same time, they would use their *reatas,* leather ropes, to lasso the cattle. It was dangerous, for a mistake could bring a rider crashing down.

Juan handed her a sombrero. "Put this on, and tuck your hair inside," he said. "If someone recognizes you, they will tell your father."

"Papá would not mind," Luisa said.

Luisa and Juan had both been born at the same time, eleven years ago. Growing up, they had become good friends. Luisa had nine brothers and sisters, but they were all older. She felt as close to Juan as if he were a brother.

Together, they walked to the stables. Juan had two horses waiting. Luisa patted hers, a gray filly named Estrella.

She led Estrella into the corral. Standing on the lower rail of the fence, Luisa pulled herself into the saddle. She had worn *chaparrales,* leather pants to protect her legs against brush.

As Juan led the way, they rode eastward. Luisa could see a touch of pink in the sky. The sun would soon rise.

Luisa saw the light of a fire. The smell of corn tortillas made her hungry. As she and Juan got closer, she saw Paiute women kneading the dough. Vaqueros stood waiting for breakfast.

Juan got two tortillas. He handed one to Luisa. The vaqueros mounted their horses. Everyone ate as they rode.

The silver spurs of the riders gleamed in the yellow dawn. The light brought out the bright colors of their shirts. The horses began to snort and neigh. They, too, knew this was a special day.

Not long after, Juan pointed toward three old, twisted cypress trees. There was a small group of cattle under the trees.

The vaqueros rode forward, shouting and whistling. The cows had just awakened and didn't want to move. But after they started, they kept going.

A visitor had once asked Luisa's father how many cattle he had. He did not like to brag, he said, but there were about 50,000.

It was not necessary to round up all the cattle. Perhaps a thousand or so would be enough for several months. That would provide food and leather for trading. It would also feed all the people on the hacienda.

Luisa and Juan followed as the vaqueros gathered up more cattle. Sometimes, one of the cows wandered away from the herd. A vaquero would ride after it and bring it back.

Once, Luisa was near a cow that turned away. She nudged Estrella toward the cow and tried to turn it back to the herd. Juan shouted at the cow. Between them, they got it back to the herd!

Finally, the herd was large enough. Some of the vaqueros turned the cattle around. They headed for the corral. Others rode on, looking for more cows.

"Which way do you want to go?" Juan asked
Luisa.

"To the corral," she said.

Luisa wanted to watch the vaqueros use their
reatas there. She admired their skill with the
long cowhide rope.

The vaqueros drove the cattle into a large corral. They started the cattle moving in a large circle. Some of the best reata handlers rode forward. They worked in pairs to rope the cows.

Luisa and Juan watched as the vaqueros went about their work. The vaqueros moved swiftly. There was no time to lose.

Papá had told her that they should be grateful for the cows. They provided almost everything the people on the hacienda needed. Their hides made clothing, shoes, saddles, and mats for the floor.

The meat would be saved to feed the dozens of people who lived on the hacienda. Some of it would be dried and preserved.

Luisa and Juan watched the vaqueros rope more cattle. Then, another group arrived with a second herd of cattle. Juan nudged Luisa. When she looked, she saw that her father was riding with the vaqueros.

"You should go," Juan said.

Luisa pulled down her sombrero to hide her face. But it was too late for that. Papá had already seen her.

"Luisa!" Papá waved at her. Slowly, she rode over to him. "Mamá has been looking for you. You did not tell anyone you would go to the rodeo."

Juan spoke up. "It is my fault, don Mariano," he said. "You should punish me."

Papá nodded. "It is brave of you to say so," he told Juan. "But I think Luisa makes up her own mind what to do."

Papá broke into a smile. Luisa knew he forgave her. "Go back now," he said. "You will see Juan at the fiesta tonight."

Luisa rode home. She ran toward the back of the house where the kitchen was. Before long, she was sitting in a tub of water, washing off the dust and dirt.

A maid had gone to her room and brought Luisa's green dress. After Luisa slipped it on, the maid brushed her hair until it shone. Finally, Luisa placed a silver necklace around her neck. Papá had given it to her for her tenth birthday, and he always liked to see it on her.

After she was ready, Luisa went out to the *terraza,* or terrace. Tables were already being set out for the fiesta. Servants carried bowls of fruit, bread, pastries, olives, and sweets. Others were preparing the pit where beef would be roasted. Mamá was there, pointing this way and that, making sure everything was just right.

At last, Mamá noticed Luisa. "Ah," she said, "where have you been hiding? There is work to be done."

"I was taking a bath, Mamá," Luisa said.

Just then, they heard the sound of a carriage.
"Guests are coming. Go and greet them," said
Mamá.

Luisa was happy to do it. After that, Mamá
forgot to ask where she had been that morning.

Night had fallen, but the candles and oil lamps made the terraza bright as day. The sounds of guitars and violins mixed with the laughter of happy people. Neighbors had come from as far as a day's ride on horseback. And one by one, the vaqueros had come to join the feasting and celebration.

Luisa watched the women and men dance. Then someone put a plate of sweet pastries down in front of her. She turned, and her eyes opened wide. It was Juan, but he was dressed in a new suit. "My mother made me wear this tonight," he said.

Luisa smiled and took one of the pastries. "You look very fine, Juan," she said. "This has been a wonderful day!"